A Forest Fire

written by Pam Holden
illustrated by Samer Hatam

The forest was on fire!

It was burning fast.

The butterflies came out.
They were flying fast.

The birds came out.
They were flying faster.

The grasshoppers came out.
They were hopping fast.

The frogs came out.
They were hopping faster.

The snails came out.
They were sliding fast.

The snakes came out.
They were sliding faster.

The rabbits came out.
They were jumping fast.

The kangaroos came out.
They were jumping faster.

The turtles came out.
They were crawling fast.

The lizards came out.
They were crawling faster.

The firefighters went in.

They were driving fast.

The fire went out.
SSSsssssss!